Prey of the Space

Wilbur S. Peacock

Alpha Editions

This edition published in 2024

ISBN 9789362092380

Design and Setting By

Alpha Editions
www.alphaedis.com

Email - info@alphaedis.com

Prey of the Space Falcon

Curt Varga watched lazily from a shadowed corner of the Martian *gailang* night club, his space-tanned left hand toying with a frosted glass of *cahnde*, and his right hand making cryptic marks with a radi-stylus upon the scrap of gold paper before him.

Music was a lilting swirl in the air, and his booted foot tapped unconsciously with the muted rhythm. He smiled at the great-chested Martians squatted about the dance floor, wondering for the hundredth time what enjoyment they received from swaying to music they understood only as a series of harmonic vibrations.

Over by the circular bar, four Venusians drank stiffly and stolidly of Venusian *cahnde*, as they stood knee-deep in their water tanks. Their skins were wet and slimy, eternally soaked with the fluids flowing from the glands in their reptilian skins. They watched the good-natured crowd from beneath nictilian lids, their gazes blank and eerily aloof.

Curt Varga's throat muscles tightened as he sent his inaudible questions to his brother in the curtained booth across the room.

"Is there any suspicion that you are working with me?" he asked. "If so, then this arrangement must be broken; I can't ruin your career, too."

The bean-sized amplifier imbedded so cunningly in the living bone at his right temple vibrated lightly from the mocking laughter.

"I think they do, Falcon," Val Varga said lightly. "But it doesn't matter; somebody has to do the undercover work—and I happen to be in a position where I can do it with the least suspicion." The voice softened. "Careers *aren't* important, anyway. I seem to remember that Dad had quite a reputation as a bio-chemist, until the Food Administrators decided his work threatened their dictatorial monopoly. And as a Commander of the IP, you were slated to go rather high."

Curt Varga grinned, and suddenly all of the deadly grimness was gone from his tanned face, and there was only the laughter in his cool grey eyes and the hint of a swashbuckling swagger to the tilt of his head to betoken the man.

"OQ!" he said inaudibly into the amplifier unit. "Now, give me a few facts."

"Well," Val's voice steadied, "the IP is still searching for the Falcon's base; they've got direct orders from Vandor to smash it within a month, Earth time. The situation is getting rather desperate; gardens have been found on half a dozen worlds, and the revenue from sale of vitamins and energy tablets has fallen alarmingly. Unless the base is found and destroyed, the IP is due for a general shake-up in command and personnel."

"Hold it!" Curt said brusquely, glanced at the Martian waiter who padded along the wall toward him.

The waiter, grotesquely-chested, round-headed, with his antennae curled on either side of his great single eye, threaded his way through the tables, stood solicitously over the Falcon's table. His right antennae uncurled, its tip lightly darting out to touch the Earthman's wrist.

"Another *cahnde*," Curt Varga said loudly. "And a *pulnik* capsule."

"*Five IP agents just entered*," the Martian said, the nerve impulse emanating from the antennae and travelling along Curt's arm to his brain, where the impulse was changed into familiar English. "*I think they know you are here.*"

"Thank you, Yen Dal," the Falcon said evenly. "That will do fine."

He leaned indolently back in his chair, his clear gaze utterly guileless, a lazy hint of careless laughter lifting the corners of his mobile lips. He tightened the muscles of his belly, shifting the gun-belt a bit until the dis-gun lay flat along his thigh. He felt mocking laughter bubbling in his throat, when he saw the IP men moving inconspicuously about the night club, their keen gaze searching patiently and eagerly every shadowed corner. The Martian padded silently away.

"Things are getting hot, Val," he said into his throat mike. "Yen Dal just told me that five IP men are searching the place. Better get out of here before a fight starts."

"I heard your conversation." Val's voice grew tight and hurried. "Now listen, Curt," he finished. "As far as I have been able to learn, the headquarters of the *Smothalene* Smugglers lies somewhere in the Sargasso. An Earth renegade, Duke Ringo, is the boss. You've got to smash those smugglers, and do it quickly, for the worlds are beginning to believe that the Falcon is the man behind the *smothalene* smuggling."

Curt Varga scowled unconsciously, swirled the liquid about in the bottom of his *cahnde* glass. He felt the first pulsings of anger in his heart, and his grey eyes were no longer cool.

"I know," he answered brittlely. "Two of my ships rocketed into a trap on Jupiter's moons last week. They were carrying cargoes of oranges to the *Dahkils*, and some woman whose son had died of *smothalene* gave information to the IP."

"I hadn't heard that," Val said slowly, his voice grave.

"Now, here's the situation," the Falcon said tautly, watching the unhurried movements of an IP man walking along the long bar. "I have sold almost enough fruit and vegetables the past three months to finance buying three more Kent-Horter needle-rockets. My fleet is almost complete, lacking but a dozen or so ships that I figure will be the minimum needed to whip the IP. I won't contact you again here, but will let you know where to meet me later. This place is getting too hot; I've got a hunch somebody tipped the fact that I use this as headquarters on Mars. Get out of here as inconspicuously as you can; then I'll make a run for it, if necessary."

"OQ, Curt!" Val's voice with subdued. "But take it easy; your job is too big to be destroyed because you insist on taking chances."

"Forget it, kid."

The Falcon finished the liquor in the first glass, sipped slowly at the fresh *cahnde* set before him by a noiseless waiter. Deep in his mind sang a tiny warning voice of danger. But he sat still, waiting for an opportunity to make a silent escape from the night club that was fast becoming an IP trap. His keen gaze flicked about the room, finding and identifying the agents scattered through the crowd.

He broke the *pulnik* capsule, rolled the fragrant tobacco in a fresh paper, lit it with his pocket lighter. He smoked slowly, the glow shadowing the flat planes of his face, lighting the rugged, almost brutal, sweep of his jaw. He edged his chair back quietly, tensing the great muscles of his legs, estimated the distance to the rear door.

Other than that, he didn't move, for he saw that he was watched by two agents converging on him from both sides of the swaying dancers on the floor. He smiled slightly, sat cool and debonair, the leather vest and silk singlet accenting the wedge of his deep chest and shoulders.

"*Any minute now, Val*," he said into his throat amplifier.

The *Kaana* four-piece orchestra swung into the soft lazy melody of a century before. Glasses clinked at the bar, and the soft rustle of laughing conversation made the room seem intimate and warm. Nostalgia bit at Curt Varga's heart, when he remembered the days not so many years before when his life had been an ordered thing, when he had not been a hunted outlaw prowling the spaceways, a price on his head.

In those days, before his mind had fully matured, he had thought his life full and untrammelled. He had worn his uniform as an IP Commander with the bullying swagger his superiors affected. With dis-guns and a brutal carelessness, he had enforced the commands of Jason Vandor, Dak Yar and Mezo Yong, the Food Administrators, had forced obedience from recalcitrant people of a dozen worlds, had been the leader of the shock-troops that pillaged city after city because they had incurred the anger of the Triumvirate whose hands controlled the food supplies of the Solar System.

Then in his twenty-fifth year, he had seen the foulness of the system that broke the lives and courage of the inhabitated worlds. He had seen his father blasted to death for daring to raise his voice against the tyranny of the Food Administrators. He had seen his older brother die while fighting to save their father. And a conflict had raged within him for days; he had fought against the training that had been instilled within him from the day of his birth.

From musty records, he had reread the histories of the worlds, had really *understood* for the first time the true meaning of freedom. And in that hour, he had thrown aside all that had been his life, and had striven to build a new one. In a stolen Kent-Horter, he had prowled the spaceways, striking at small freighters for supplies and wealth. In the cold of space, he had stooped like the Falcon for whom he had been named, and stolen the Food Administrators' supplies time and again.

And as ever when a leader arises, other men and women came to him as filings are attracted to a lodestone. Some were renegades, the scum of the spacelanes, whose only desire was to pillage and rob those who could not fight back. But others were the peoples of a dozen worlds in whose minds flowed the desire for freedom, whose only wish was to aid in a seemingly-hopeless fight against the oppressors. And still others were the great minds of science and art and living whose lives had been stifled by rigid rules of living imposed by the Food Administrators.

Plan after plan had been made and discarded, until one was left that showed the clever brilliance of its creators. Unlimited wealth was the one thing needed for a revolution, and the plan showed clearly that way in which it could be obtained.

Because they controlled all energy-tablet and vitamin factories, the Food Administrators held a whip hand over all the worlds. Starvation was the answer to any trouble that might arise. And should the trouble become too large to handle with the starvation threat, then the degenerate remnants of the famous Interplanetary Patrol used their weapons and brutal methods to enforce the laws.

The plan reasoned out by Curt Varga and his board of strategy had been clever enough to avoid all obstacles.

In a great asteroid, used by the Falcon for his first base, great rooms had been hollowed by gargantuan dis-guns. These rooms had been converted into living quarters for the men and women. Once established there, the men and women had worked for two years to hollow out more caverns for the growing of fruit and vegetables by hydropony. Still more rooms were manufactured for the workshops and hangars for the fitting of a huge space fleet with which the Falcon hoped to smash for all time the IP and the three men who controlled it.

And in the passing four years the gigantic task had almost reached fruition. Dead-black freighters raced the starways, carrying contraband food to all planets, there unloading, and then returning with all monies collected to buy more space equipment for the fight that was to come.

The Falcon's luck had been phenomenal; he had lost less than two percent of his men and fleet since the day his plans had been carefully organized. While IP ships had been blasted out of existence at the alarming rate of over five per cent a year.

Of course there had been trouble. There had been the internal revolution created by the rotten elements of his pirate gang. Blood had been spilled, and the war had been a deadly one that lasted for ninety days. Then the Falcon's men had conquered the others by clever maneuvering, had quashed the civil war at the cost of hundreds of lives. Telepathy and hypnotism had been used on all of the survivors, driving all thoughts of greed from their minds, fitting their mentalities for the task that was a common purpose.

And there had been the time when the IP had almost closed a trap over the Food Smugglers' leaders. Only a lucky chance had sprung the trap too soon, permitting Curt Varga and most of his board of strategy to escape.

But those things lay in the past. Now a new situation had arisen that promised to be more destructive to their plans than any IP plot or internal strife.

Smothalene smugglers had begun to operate again on each planet. Once, the drug had been outlawed, all sources of the Venusian *lanka* plant, from which it was derived, had been blasted from existence. But now the drug had reappeared, was being smuggled from some secret base, and its origin could not be found.

The inhabitated worlds were slowly becoming convinced that the Falcon and his men were distributing the drug; and such was the horror and agony the drug inflicted on its users, the peoples of the worlds had forgotten the good done by the Falcon's men, and were giving information to the IP as to the movements of the Food Smugglers.

It had become a war of survival for the Falcon; he had to stamp out the *smothalene* smugglers so as to protect himself, his great plan, and the lives of those who had entrusted their futures to his capable hands.

Progress had been slow, for the *smothalene* ring had been so carefully organized that only the barest of information was obtainable. But Curt Varga's organization, too, was carefully organized. His spies and agents had been working for weeks, ferreting out trivial bits of information, then relaying it back to headquarters where it was sifted and fitted with exquisite skill and patience.

For days, the Falcon had prowled the planets, contacting his agents, obtaining first-hand reports, doing two men's work himself. Now, he had the clue given him by his brother, and he felt a thrill of success touching his mind as he thought over his plans for invading the Sargasso of Space, where the drug ring's headquarters were supposed to be.

But the pressing problem of the moment was not the *smothalene* smugglers, but rather the saving of himself from the IP men who were advancing so grimly on his table.

The Falcon shifted his glance indolently about the room, giving only an uninterested cursory scrutiny to the agents, then relaxed, his cigarette canted debonairly between his lips. He glanced about in faked surprise, when one of the agents seated himself at the table.

"What the hell do you want?" he asked pleasantly. "There are plenty of empty tables; when I want company, I'll send out invitations!"

The agent said nothing; his eyes made a quick inventory of Curt's lounging body, widening imperceptibly when they saw the casual wornness of the dis-gun's butt. He nodded at his companion, and the man ranged himself at the Falcon's left side.

Curt Varga straightened, feigning anger. "Listen," he said coldly, "I don't know you, so beat it!"

The agent at the table opened his hand; a small shield glowed dully in the palm. "What's your number, Earthman?" he asked heavily.

The Falcon shrugged, held out his wrist. The agent standing beside the table lifted a pocket fluorscope tube, trained it on the exposed wrist. The flesh seemed to dissolve, and numbers glowed bluely from the ulna bone.

"X three five one four eight L T," the agent read impersonally. He twitched off the fluorscope beam; the flesh magically came back into being. The second agent spoke the numerals and letters into a pocket vocoder.

"Hell," the Falcon said, "why didn't you tell me you were IP men? I haven't done anything wrong!"

"Who are you, and why the gun?"

Curt Varga shrugged. "I'm a scavenger, just in for a couple of days. I always carry a gun; I've got a permit from the IP here on Mars." He dry-washed his hands nervously. "Look, I don't want any trouble; I'll help any way I can, if you'll tell me what you want."

"Shut up!" the seated agent said brittlely, listened to the tinny voice coming from his vocoder. Then he pocketed the tiny unit, stood slowly. "Your numbers check," he said slowly. "But don't leave this place without my permission."

Without another word, he and his partner walked back to the bar. Curt Varga sat silently for a moment, feeling the cold sweat on his spine, breathing a bit fast. He grinned slightly, mockingly, remembering the hours of pain that had been his when the surgeons of his hidden base had grafted the ulna of a slain Earthman into his arm after removing the natural bone. Unconsciously, his right hand lifted, and the forefinger traced the invisible scars left on his face by the surgeon whose plastic surgery had changed the shape of his features.

"I think I passed all right, Val," he said into the microphone imbedded in the cartilage of his throat. "Take it easy."

"OQ, Curt," Val answered. "I'm about to get the once over, too."

The Falcon's fingers dipped into his pocket, found a bill. He laid it on the table, came lithely to his feet. He stood there for silent seconds, watching the crowd that swayed to the music.

Then he walked toward the bar; and there was in the unconscious swagger of his stride a love of life and laughter, a hint of the adventurer's blood that made his home the great sweeps of starway that stretched to the far horizons of the universe.

He skirted the swaying dancers on the dance floor, thrust out a steadying hand to the weaving figure of a Martian *boiloong* who had evidently been inhaling *gailang* gas for too long a period in the rooms below. The *boiloong* embraced him drunkenly with a couple of tentacles, then staggered benignly away, hiccoughing loudly from two of his three mouths.

"*Cahnde*," Curt said to the bartender. The music piled in tiny swirls of melody in the air, and he absently hummed several notes of it. He accepted the frosted glass from the bartender, turned, braced his elbows on the bar. He stood silently, his nerves like taut wire.

He watched the crowd, permitting his eyes to lift to the alcove in which his brother sat. He felt a surge of affection for the man who dared to fight at his side for a principle he did not clearly understand. They met but once or twice a year, and then surreptitiously, for Val was on the chemi-staff of the Food Administrators' greatest vitamin plant. They knew they played a deadly game, in which the probable reward was death; but such was the mettle of the brothers, they gave no heed.

An IP agent jerked the curtain aside on the booth, spoke to the seated man. The Falcon could barely make out the words, the speech coming through the amplifier grafted into Val's throat, as they were grafted into all key man of the Falcon's brood.

"Declare yourself," the agent snapped.

"Jak Denton, five four three M R S two nine, on special furlough from the chemi-staff at Luhr." Val Varga's voice was submissive, resigned, as befitted those who knew the power of the IP.

Tiny sparks of anger flared in the depths of the Falcon's grey eyes, and the muscles swelled across his wide back. But he made no outward move. "It checks," he heard the agent declare a moment later, and then the agent stepped from the booth.

The Falcon smiled slightly, drank slowly from his glass. Then his fingers tightened spasmodically, and he felt shock traveling over his lithe body in a nerve-tightening shroud.

"Get out of here, Val," he snapped earnestly into his throat-mike. "The showdown is coming."

Time was frozen for the moment. The music dwindled to flat discords, and the dancers were only a blur at the edge of his line of sight. The Falcon straightened, set the glass on the bar without turning around, and braced his wide-spread booted feet. He felt a surge of fear in his heart, and the muscles of his gun hand were tight and strained. He knew then that the trap was sprung; it was too late to run.

Yen Dal, the Martian waiter, was on his knees, his mouth gaping in soundless agony, held there by a numbing paralysis beam in the hands of the IP man who had questioned Curt. His single eye rolled in the ecstasy of pain, and his antennae twisted and writhed with an uncanny life, as the paralysis beam ripped along each nerve with exquisite agony. Then a whistle of pain came from his lung orifice, scaled until it was almost inaudible—and his body threshed in an intolerable spasm that was horrible to see.

The Falcon stepped from the bar, circled noiselessly toward the rear exit, felt panic eating at his nerves, for he knew that Yen Dal could not hold out much longer.

He stopped in the shadow of a pillar, seeing the IP agent beside the door. He turned a bit, gasped, when he saw that the paralysis beam had been turned off, and that the Martian's antennae was wrapped tightly about the agent's wrist. Then the agent whirled, and his shrill whistle ripped the music to scattered shreds.

"*Get that man!*" he bellowed. "*He's the Falcon!*"

Curt Varga went whirling to one side, and the dis-gun leaped into his fingers. A needle-ray brushed at his back, and he scythed the agent down with a withering blast from the dis-gun. Smoke surged from a naming drapery, where a ray slashed, and then the curtain flaked into nothingness.

A Venusian screamed in a high thin whistle, dropped below the surface of the water in which he stood. The music stilled in broken fragments, and women screamed their fear in panic-stricken voice. Vibrations from a hundred sets of antennae filled the air with a solid sense of knowing dread.

"Shoot that man!" the first agent screamed again, and his voice died in a choking burbling sound, as the Falcon's shot caught him squarely in the throat.

Curt fired without conscious thought, his hand following the dictates of instinctive thinking, the blazing energy of his gun's discharges hissing in a blurred stream at the agents firing from behind pillars and overturned tables.

An agent came erect, sighed deliberately, died, his head blown completely from his shoulders by a shot winging from a side booth.

"Get out of here, Curt!" Val Varga's voice rang high and exalted. "I'll keep them busy."

His gun sang again in his hand, and there was something simple and heroic about the manner in which he stood before the booth on his crippled twisted legs. He was not a cripple then, not the remnant of a man the IP had crushed and left for dead years before when he had stood fighting at his father's side. He was, instead, bright and formidable, like the licking blade of a cause that fought against superstitious greed and intolerance.

"This is my way, Falcon," he called clearly. "Don't let me down."

Curt Varga sobbed deep in his throat, seeing that last gallant stand of the man whose deformities and keen brain had made him able to act as a spy in the Food Adminstrators' stronghold. He spun on his heel, smashed a Martian to one side with a sweep of his gun-hand, then rayed an agent to death with a brutal callousness utterly foreign to his nature.

He plowed through the tables, scattering them and their screaming occupants, hoping to get to his brother's side before the man was killed. He cursed in a vicious steady whisper, darted through the crowd, firing without sighting at the men behind him. He ducked instinctively, and a network of rays crossed the spot where his head had been, burning the very air, filling all the room with the stench of ozone.

And then he was at Val's side, towering over him, and their guns wove a barrage before whom Death walked with a steady implacable stride.

An IP agent screamed, pawed blindly at the shattered remains of his face, his gun singing an undirected arc of death about the room. Bodies were lanced with the ray, and the cries of the dead made a ghastly overtone to the sound of the firing.

And then Val sagged, caught through the chest with a ray bolt that held him erect for a fleeting moment. He fell, his free hand clutching Curt's arm, almost dragging him from his feet. He smiled a bit as he died, and his voice was barely audible.

"*Make it a good world, Curt,*" he said, and he was dead.

The Falcon straightened, and there was no mercy in his eyes then; there was only a bleak grief and a hate for those whose utter blind stupidity and cruelty had brought about such a situation.

He went forward lightly, his gun blazing in his hand, his face craggy and stone-like. He never looked back at the huddle which had been his brother.

An IP man died in a blast of searing energy that sought him out behind a pillar, surging through the wood, and then withering him into a charred and blackened mass. Another agent turned to run, and the bolt of Curt's dis-gun skewered his back, pinned him to a wall for a fleeting second, then dropped him in a silent heap.

Curt whirled, darted toward the rear door. His gun menaced the entire room, and he was a shifting fading figure as he fled from that room of death. His eyes were blurred with tears, and his throat was constricted with grief. At the door, he hesitated briefly, then surged ahead. He heard the shrill whistles of other IP men in the street before the night club, and his nerves were tense for the slightest of sounds betokening hidden watchers in the alleyway.

He slammed the door behind him, raced down the alley. He tripped, rolled like a prowling cat, came lithely to his feet again. His hand brushed at a wall to steady himself, missed its hold, and he lurched to one side.

That misstep saved his life. A blazing bolt from a dis-rifle sprayed molten rock from the alley's floor, swung, tried to catch him in its range. He fired twice, shooting instinctively, feeling a gladness in him when he heard the choking death-rattle of the man who had fired.

He twisted about a corner, ran with a desperate speed, hearing the growing sounds of pursuit behind. He knew a place of comparative safety a block away, and he plunged toward it through the moon-lit night.

Feet were pounding in the street, when he came to a manhole that led into the unused conduit system of the city. He knew he was watched but he knew also that he had to make his escape as best he could. He kicked the rusted latch of the manhole cover free, lifted the lid, shoved one leg through. Sitting on the manhole rim, he lifted his other leg through the hole, then braced his hands, and lowered himself so fast he almost fell.

The single shot melted the edge of the conduit opening, flecked briefly at the side of his head, dropped him squarely into a blaze of flame that seemed to grow out of nowhere and fold him in its embrace.

II

The Falcon landed in a sprawling heap, cramped with vertigo, his mind numb with the shock of the shot that had slapped at the side of his head. He groped blindly for support, felt the skin ripping from his hands on the rough metal of the pipe. For seconds, he fought to retain his senses, finally forced the black shadow of unconsciousness back from his mind.

His eyes focused slowly, made out the glow cast through the open manhole. Only a moment could have passed, for he still heard the excited calling of his pursuers, and felt the vibrations of men climbing the outside of the pipe.

He went at a staggering run down the pipe, guiding himself by the beam of the radi-light torch he fumbled from his belt. Echoes drummed along the metal tube from his running feet, and the dull pounding in his head raced with the sound. He whirled around a bend in the pipe, stopped, braced himself momentarily on the curved wall. Then, the ringing in his head slowing, and his mind clearing, he ran again at a faster pace.

The yells of his pursuers rocketed through the tube, slowly gaining. But a thin smile twisted the Falcon's mouth; he had a bolt-hole or two that were unknown to any but him, holes that had saved his life before.

He slipped now and then in the greasy seepage at the pipe's bottom, came again to his feet, feeling strength draining from him, realizing that the shot had almost put a partial stasis on his nervous system.

He ran slower now, utterly unable to keep up the headlong pace. His breath was hot and dry in his throat, and a heart-pain in his side cramped his belly. He staggered again and again, until at last he could move only at a fast walk.

The agents gained, crying their pack call like Martian *ganths* running a lowland creature to death in a canal bottom. Their boots slammed driving echoes from the pipe, growing louder with each passing second.

The Falcon knew that he could run no further; he leaned against the wall, checked the charge in his gun. A mirthless laugh grated in his throat, and he felt futility beating at his heart for the first time in years.

"*Make it a good world, Curt!*" Val had said.

Curt Varga fought then, fought the dizziness in his mind, struggled with the defeat he felt in his heart. He had a task to do; not for himself, not for his martyred brothers and father—but for a dozen worlds to whom he and his brood had become a symbol of hope in a blackened century.

He spun about, seeking a manhole opening, saw none. He did not know where he was, for there were no identifying marks in the tube. He thought swiftly, but his thoughts seemed to move with a treacly slowness. Then he lifted his gun, flicked it to full force, blasted a hole through the side of the conduit.

Metal flowed in a crimson stream, grew turgid, hardened with the queerness of the native iron. Great blisters reared on the Falcon's hands as he clawed his way from the tube. He fell to the ground outside, blinked, tried to find his directions by some distinctive landmark. He gasped, whirled back to the pipe.

He had come squarely into the parking plaza at the rear of the spaceport at the edge of the city. Before him, guards had whirled, were running toward him, already clawing for the guns at their waists. And even as he turned, he heard the excited cries of the agents inside the conduit pipe.

He ran at a zig-zag pace, hugging the shadow of the pipe, toward a fleet tiny cruiser rolling into its parking place. Darting across a cleared space of ground, he tugged at the inset port-handle.

The port surged open from the weight of the air-pressure inside, and the Falcon dived through, pulling the port shut again. Still in a crouch, he spun the gun in his hand, jammed it into the side of the single passenger.

"Get out of here," he snarled. "Gully-hop this ship—and do it fast."

"Listen, you—" the pilot began.

"Either you do—or I do. Now, get going." The Falcon's face was utterly bleak and cruel, his eyes blazing with the trapped lust of a cornered wolf.

Shots slammed against the impervium hull, bounced harmlessly away. The vizi-screen glowed greenly, and the reflection of the Port Authority appeared.

"*Take off, and we'll ray you down.*"

The Falcon growled deep in his throat, slammed into the dual control seat, snapped the control-switch to his side. With a single twitch of his right hand, he sent the ship flipping skyward.

The cruiser whipped through the night, inertia momentarily pinning its passengers to their seats. A beam lanced out from the spaceport, instantly winked off. The Falcon's hands made lightning adjustments on the board, and the ship scooted back toward the ground, fled, barely a hundred feet above the rusty sand.

The vizi-screen was dull now, reflecting the interior of the port office—and the Port Authority's voice sang through the speaker.

"Five IP ships take off. Catch that pleasure cruiser. Use tractors to bring it down; it isn't armed. Watch out for the man aboard—he's the Falcon."

"*The Falcon!*" Fear was in the voice; the words were barely breathed.

Curt Varga smiled savagely, glanced around, fully saw his companion for the first time. He felt a certain sense of amazement; but so much had happened to him in the past hour, he no longer had the capacity for complete surprise.

She was tiny, and the synthesilk dress gloved the soft curves of her body. Her nose was impudent against the red of her mouth, and fright was in her bluish-green eyes momentarily. Then she stiffened, and her eyes were hard with a calculating coldness.

"I thought kidnaping went out with the dark ages," she said quietly.

"Miss, this is *shipnapping*." Ironical humor softened the brutal harshness of Curt Varga's jaw for the moment.

And then there was no time for talk, for he was weaving the ship in a manner that only a space-master could do, flipping the cruiser about until metal sang in a dozen tones, evading the bluish rays that fingered from the ships behind.

He gained the night shadow, circled about on muffled jets, watched the IP ships flash past him in hot pursuit of their quarry. Then he sent the cruiser straight back toward the city, angling after a time toward the mountains to the north. Not a word was spoken until after he had landed the cruiser close to his own rocket hidden beneath the overhang of a rusty bluff.

"Now what?" the girl asked.

The Falcon killed the rockets, turned about on the seat, conscious for the first time that he still held his dis-gun against her side with his left hand.

He thought fast then, made plans and discarded them with a speed that raced them kaleidoscopically through his mind. He could leave the girl tied in the cruiser—but she had seen him, could identify him to the IP men. Or he could—he shrank from the thought; he was brutal in a dispassionate way, but he was no murderer.

"Get out," he snapped.

Color surged into the girl's face, then faded, leaving the skin a sickly white. She shrank from him, pressing against the far wall.

"I read it in your eyes," she whispered. "You were thinking of *killing* me!"

The Falcon flushed angrily, more at himself than at the girl, hating himself for thinking such thoughts, hating the twisted years that had warped him to the point that he acted like the scum he had weeded from among his men.

"Get out," he said again, and his voice was softer. "I mean you no harm." He flicked a glance from the port, toward the sky where the violet beams of mass-detectors probed the sky and earth.

She slid from the seat, took the two steps to the port, opened it with a surge of lithe strength. She dropped to the ground, followed by the Falcon. There was a puzzled fear in her eyes, a fear that grew by the moment as she saw the sleek Kent-Horter quiescent on the sand.

The Falcon stepped lithely about his prisoner, whistled with a queerly distorted note, and the port came automatically open. He gestured with the gun, impatience flaming in his eyes as she hesitated.

"Walk—or be carried," he warned grimly.

The girl scrambled into the pirate ship. Curt Varga stepped in behind her, dogged the door shut with almost casual flicks of his right hand. He urged the girl before him with the gun, waved her into a sleeping cubicle, then pulled the door shut, locked it.

Holstering the dis-gun, he raced to the pilot room, slid into the pilot's seat. He warmed the rockets with brief twitches of his fingers on the control studs, then pulled the drive switch a third of the way back.

He felt the thrust of the rockets against his body, saw the brief flicker of the girl's ship whipping past the port. Then his ship was fleeing with accelerating speed into the tenuous atmosphere.

A dis-cannon rolled the ship, almost sent it on beam's end. He straightened her, poured the power into the Kent converters, flicked out of range with amazing ease. Air whistled through the purifying-system, and he cut the rheostat down a bit when the reading gave an Earth-norm.

Then, and only then, did he relax. He set a reading into the calculator, flicked on the robot control, and walked slowly back to the sleeping cubicle he had momentarily made into a cell.

"Come on out, now," he said, swung the door fully open.

She had been crying, and the defiant gesture with which she tried to hide that fact built a tiny warm glow in Curt Varga's heart. But he didn't permit that feeling to show; he knew he had to keep the girl more or less cowed, if he were to have no trouble with her.

"Come on," he said again. "We'll declare a truce for the time."

She stepped past him, walked toward the pilot's room. He followed, liking her unconscious swagger which matched his own. She refused to sit, and he took one empty seat, regarded her quizzically, as he rolled a *pulnik* cigarette.

"Who are you?" he said at last.

Puzzlement kindled in the girl's eyes, was as quickly erased.

"I'm Jean—Harlon," she said slowly. She gestured about the ship. "Why did you kidnap me?"

The Falcon laughed, and youth was in his face again, some of the bitter lines softening and erasing utterly away.

"It wasn't planned," he admitted. "I was being chased—I saw your ship taxiing into a parking place—and I commandeered it." He shrugged. "You just happened to be the ship's pilot."

Amusement lifted the girl's mouth for a moment, then concern deepened the blue of her eyes. She glanced at the calculator, saw that a course had been set, and a tiny muscle twitched in her throat.

"I'm going with you!" It was a statement.

Curt Varga nodded. "Sorry," he said, "but that's the way it has to be. Only two men knew my identity—and they're dead. The few IP's who saw me tonight are also dead. It's a safety measure."

Jean Harlon stiffened slightly. "I could give my word," she said slowly.

The Falcon shook his head. "Sorry, but the stakes are too big for me to risk another's word." He nodded at the empty seat. "Sit down," he finished kindly. "In some ways, I'm not quite as bad as I am painted."

Curt Varga tensed, felt the probing finger of thought digging at his mind. He threw up a mind-shield almost casually, grinned mockingly.

"A *telepath*?" he said conversationally.

Irritation colored the girl's cheeks; then reluctant admiration came into her eyes. She accepted a *pulnik* capsule, deftly rolled a cigarette, before answering.

"Not many could dismiss me that easily," she asserted. "I had five years at NYU, on Earth." She accepted a light for the cigarette.

Curt Varga nodded. "Old habit," he disclaimed. "I used to play space-rocketry with the thought-men of Pluto; the guy with an unshielded mind never had a chance."

Jean Harlon's gaze was speculative. "What happened?" she said. "Or am I stepping on your toes?"

The Falcon's face was twisted then with a show of emotion that brought a glance of disbelief from the girl. And then resolve flared in the set of his shoulders, and his voice was steady.

"I was making agent-contacts. One of my men must have tipped the IP, for they came into my 'headquarters' and made a quiet search. I would have got away, but for the fact they used that diabolic paralysis beam on a friend of mine. He pointed me out." Curt shrugged. "I had to fight my way from the trap. My brother was killed. I escaped through the conduit system, came out on the spaceport. You know the rest."

"Your brother was killed!" Loathing was in Jean Harlon's eyes. "And you can sit there, and talk calmly about it?"

Anger and grief unsteadied the Falcon's voice for a moment.

"What the hell should I do—beat my chest and swear vengeance! Val knew the cards were stacked against us; he knew that both of us had lived past our appointed times. He played the game as he saw it, and died with few regrets. Hell, yes, I can talk calmly; now I've got a job to do, I've got to finish the thing for which he and hundreds of thousands of others have died!"

He turned to the space-scanner, saw that the Kent-Horter had escaped the IP ships, felt the burning of unshed tears in his eyes. He sat silently for a moment, then whipped about as the girl's words caught at his mind.

"—dreaming fools," she was saying. "What *more* could they ask than they already have. They eat, they sleep, they have amusements and medical care. Their lives are as perfect as science can make them."

"*Science!*" Curt Varga's tone flicked like a whip-lash. "You can't run people's lives as though they were bits of unfeeling machinery. Every man has the right to control his own destiny."

Anger was in Jean Harlon's face then, too. "You blind atavistic fool," she blazed, "people cannot rule themselves! Read your histories, find in them the truth about self-government. Why, until science took the reins of power, millions died in ghastly wars for fanatical leaders whose greed for world dictatorial power was an insane fixation."

The Falcon's face was like chiseled granite. He silenced the girl with a brief motion of his hand. His voice was grave with the strength of his heart-felt belief in the thing he had made his life.

"I have no desire to convert you," he said quietly. "Conversion comes to but a few. You've got to know deep in your heart that what I say is the truth. There were wars, holocausts started by the mad dictators of the

Twentieth Century. But when they were over, then democracy began to win the long struggle that had always been hers. And although other wars came through the years, always life became better for all peoples. But then science became a *master* instead of a *servant*, and the few rulers of science became the rulers of the universe. That would have been all right, had the rule been a beneficient one—but it was twisted and distorted by the descendants of our hereditary Food Administrators until it throttled and murdered all initiative and ambition and free-thinking. It strangled God-given *freedom*."

Curt Varga went suddenly silent, feeling the red creeping upward from his collar. He avoided the girl's eyes, crushed out the still butt of his cigarette.

"Sorry," he said. "I guess speech-making is getting to be a habit."

Jean Harlon did not move, but her eyes searched every plane of the pirate's face.

"You really *believe* that, don't you?" she said wonderingly.

"I do!" The Falcon's voice was calm. "And so do millions of others throughout the planets. And soon the day will come when all peoples shall rule themselves. I'm not the man who will bring about the change; I am but the nucleus, that about which the change is centered. When I am gone, another will take my place, and another, and another, until people shall be free, their eyes to the sun."

Jean Harlon moved slowly, breaking the Falcon's words. There was neither belief nor disbelief in her eyes; there was only the warm awareness that before her sat a man whose heart held an ideal and his mind a plan.

"You are a strange man, Falcon," she breathed. "But you're not quite the same as I had pictured you in my mind. Oddly enough, I am not afraid of you now."

Curt Varga grinned. "That's a point in my favor, anyway," he said. "I've never kidnapped a girl before; I wasn't certain just what I'd have to do to calm you." He shrugged. "You will go through a certain amount of discomfort," he finished, "but you will be safe—and I'll notify your family of your safety."

Jean Harlon's eyes were suddenly hooded. "I have no relatives," she admitted. "So I'll just string along with you, until you realize I'm perfectly harmless and permit me to return to Earth or Mars."

"That will be—" the Falcon began, then whipped about to the port, as the ship rocked as though shaken by a gust of wind.

"What's wrong?" Jean asked anxiously, peered out, too. "Why, it's a tractor beam—coming from that bare asteroid!"

"Watch!" the Falcon said quietly.

The pale-green beam lanced like a misty cone from the rough surface of a craggy boulder that sprang upward from the asteroid like a towering skyscraper. The pocked, rubbled surface of the asteroid glittered metallically in the faint sun-glow, great rocky spires rearing fantastically, mountainous boulders perched in reckless confusion over the pitted surface of the ground.

Weight was almost instantly doubled in the ship, as the tractor beam caught the ship in its grip. Curt adjusted the gravity shield to counteract the beam's force on himself and Jean. The rockets had stopped their steady drumming, and the Falcon explained.

"It's a variation of the standard inertia-tractor beam. Energy of flight is nullified by the inertia beam, which neutralizes all rocket power. And the tractor beam is swinging us toward the asteroid."

Jean shivered. "It happened so fast!" she said slowly.

The seconds slipped by, and there was the sensation of falling. The cruiser swung more and more toward the great boulder, descending swiftly. There was no sound, only the steady dragging of gravity on the ship from the pale beam. Absently, the Falcon cleared the board before him, cutting all switches.

And then a giant hole flowed open in the top of the huge boulder, and the pirate ship was whisked into a slanting radi-lighted tunnel.

"*Hollow!*" Jean said. "So this is the Pirate's Base!" She frowned. "But if it is hollow, why doesn't gravitic stress rip it to pieces?"

The Falcon still peered from the port. "We use a neutron-weld invented by Schutler. Using the weld, the skin of the Base could be but a foot thick, and still would not rupture nor permit the atmosphere to leak."

"Schutler! But he was executed five years ago."

Curt Varga shook his head. "No, Schutler is still alive; his twin brother took his place before the firing squad."

Horror was in the girl's eyes. "You mean that you *forced* him to sacrifice his life?"

The Falcon's tone was grimly brooding. "A man does what he thinks is right."

"But such a thing *isn't right*," Jean Harlon said defiantly.

Curt Varga turned, his face like chiseled granite. "Do you know why Schutler was sentenced to be executed?"

"Of course—treason."

The Falcon's grin was raw savagery.

"He invented a growth-stimulator which brought plants to full maturity in five days from seed-planting. The Food Administrators' empire might have toppled."

Jean Harlon stepped back, anger in her face. "I don't believe it," she declared. "I happen to know the true factor."

The Falcon shrugged, glanced again through the port. Slowly the anger fled Jean's face—and a brooding puzzlement remained.

The cruiser settled with a tiny jar, lurched slightly, came to rest. Metal rasped outside, and the entrance port began to open. The Falcon came from his seat, nodded toward the port.

"Was that the truth?" Jean Harlon asked.

"Of course! I have no reason for lying. Now, let's get out of here; I've a report to make."

Three men waited outside the open port; and the first, a massive bearded giant, caught Curt in a casual hug that whitened his smeared face.

"You lucky devil!" he roared. "Been in another scrap—and got away by the skin of your teeth. Damn, but I'd like a good fight!"

The Falcon grinned, shoved his way from the giant's arms.

"Damn it, Schutler," he snapped affectionately, "you'll kill me some day with those hugs of yours!"

Schutler laughed, tugged at his beard. "Come on," he said. "I've got an experi—"

"Wait a minute, squirt," the second man said. "Now, listen, Curt, did you make the contacts you—"

The negro brushed the others impatiently aside, tugged at Curt's arm. He smiled, and his teeth were a solid bar of white across ebony.

"Come on with me, Boss," he ordered. "You've got some cleaning up to do."

"Dammit, Curt—" Schutler began petulantly.

"Curt, those reports mus—" the second man said impatiently.

The Falcon gestured wearily. "That can wait for a time, Crandal. Right now, I need food and a bit of medical care." He grinned. "Anyway, I've a guest to show around the Base."

"A guest?" Schutler asked.

"Come out, Jean," Curt Varga called. Jean Harlon stepped from the lock, utterly lovely and feminine. She stared with puzzled eyes at the men standing with the Falcon.

"Why do you *permit* such liberties with the men you rule?" she asked.

Schutler laughed delightedly, the sound rolling and booming. "A new convert, Curt?" he said, then laughed again, and swept the startled girl into the circle of his arms. "Welcome to the snake's den," he finished happily.

Jean gasped in amazement, fought unsuccessfully to free herself from the burly arms, then subsided in a gale of infectious laughter. The Falcon grinned, tugged her free.

"You've met Schutler," he said. "This bald-headed old space-buzzard is Crandal, better known as the Encyclopedia. And this other is Jericho Jones, my number one mate."

The wizened man bobbed his head nervously. "Glad to know you, Miss," he said. "Now, Curt, about those reports."

"Howdedo, Miss," Jericho said, smiled toothily.

Schutler shoved forward. "How was the kid brother, Curt? Is he still dishing out the—" His voice trailed away, his gaze flicking about the group. "Sorry, Curt," he finished gently. "He was a good man."

The Falcon swallowed painfully, forced a smile, wincing a bit from the hands of the men where they touched his arms.

"He made his choice," he said slowly, and the words were like an eulogy.

He shrugged. "Take Jean to the women's quarters, Schutler," he finished unemotionally. "Later, she and I will dine together." He made an almost imperceptible gesture with one hand, and the giant's eyes widened in surprise.

"Sure, Curt," Schutler agreed. "We'll walk part-way with you."

"I don't think—" Jean began, then fell silent.

The Falcon grinned. "Everything's under control," he said reassuringly. "There are plenty of Earth women there. They'll fix you up with clothes or whatever you need."

"Thank you, Falcon," Jean said, but fear was flickering again in her blue-green eyes.

They walked down a gentle ramp, crossed on a suspended walk to a web-tier that hugged one wall of the gigantic room. Jean peered about in quiet excitement, open amazement in her face when she saw the hundreds of fighting ships cradled in rows. She watched the men that worked with a methodical thoroughness upon the gleaming hulls, fitting the coppery muzzles of space-cannon into place. Carts darted here and there on soundless wheels, carrying supplies to piles that never grew, because other men immediately and without hurry emptied the piles in steady streams into the holds of waiting ships.

Long radi-light tubes striped the ceiling three hundred feet overhead, filled the room with the clear yellow glow of Earth sunlight. There was an air of competence and efficiency about the scene that was compellingly impressive.

"A *throg*!" Jean gasped in sudden terror.

Curt glanced down at the spider man who minced daintily along on his fragile hairy legs. His double-facetted eyes glanced toward the suspension-walk, and two of his legs lifted in salute. A piercing vibrational whistle followed. Curt grinned, whistled an answer in a series of flatted notes, waved.

"That's Lilth," he explained. "He's a good guy, even if he is a Ganymedian. His family starved to death because they could not mine enough *xalthium*." He gestured toward a gigantic slug inching along the floor, pulling a loaded cart. "That's a Venusian *gastod*," he finished. "He is utterly helpless and harmless. He is also the only *gastod* not in captivity. His race exuded pure vitamin K from their bodies, so the Food Administrators imprisoned the entire race. He is a pirate here and does what he can—for oddly enough he has a brain and a soul."

They had crossed the bridge and walked slowly down a lighted tunnel. The tube debouched into a great amphitheater, at the mouth of which the group halted for a moment. Shouts, whistles, hissings came from the groups of men before them. In a gigantic pool of steaming water, Venusian reptile-men swam with loud splashing. On the field at the right of the pool,

Earthmen played space-ball, their tiny hand-tractors lancing pale-green rays at a floating gravity-neutralized sphere. The beams made a network of power that spun the copper ball like an air bubble in a whirlpool.

Spider men sat side by side, curling their legs beneath their globular bodies, then nipping them out again, a few at a time. Gravely they compared the numbers flipped out, then paid their wagers from piles of money at their sides.

Cat men from the tombs of Mars played Martian chess with their traditional enemies, the big-chested Upland *boiloongs* whose tentacles were like living ropes of steel. Creatures from a dozen worlds watched or played or rested, singly and in groups, about the gargantuan room.

"They're my men," The Falcon said proudly, feelingly. "And regardless of body-form, each is a *man.* They're the Falcon's Brood."

He led the way again, returning hearty greetings in a dozen tongues, waving, laughing, answering a hundred questions. At the edge of the room, near a tunnel's mouth, he turned to the girl who was strangely silent.

"I'll meet you for dinner in an hour," he promised. "Then I'll show you through the gardens."

"Fine!" Jean smiled, turned to follow the solicitous Schutler.

Crandal watched her go. "So she is not a convert," he said. "Then why bring her along?"

"She recognized me," the Falcon said simply, nodded good-bye, followed Jericho down another tunnel to his living quarters.

He walked into the three-room apartment, strode directly to the vocoder. Flicking a switch, he spoke quietly.

"A trap on Mars was set for me; have you heard any reports."

A voice answered with the methodical thoroughness of a trained agent. "Yen Dal died an hour ago of nerve shock caused by an IP's paralysis beam. The man who informed the IP was executed by our Martian agent thirty minutes later. That is all."

"Good!" the Falcon said grimly, closed the switch. He turned to the silent negro. "A *cahnde*, Jericho," he finished tiredly. "Then we'll doctor me up a bit."

He sagged in a chair, utterly spent and tired, worn from the constant strain that was his life every hour of the day. He was no longer the debonair flashing Falcon; he was only a man to whom life became grimmer and more danger-filled day by day; a man whose life was in no way his own.

III

Jean Harlon leaned back from the table, sighed blissfully.

"I never knew," she said, "that such wonderful food existed. Why, that watermelon was the most delicious thing I've eaten in my life."

Curt Varga smiled, shoved back his chair. "Let's take a quick look at the gardens before getting some sleep," he said. "I'll show you such things as the ordinary person has not seen in more than a century."

"Swell!" Jean Harlon nodded.

They walked from the dining hall, entered a side tunnel, followed a winding ramp toward the center of the asteroid. They chatted aimlessly, speaking of nothing in particular; and Curt felt a vague pleasure in him when her eyes reflected her astonishment when she found that he was educated beyond the average of most men. There was a tang to living at the moment, and his lithe body felt good and strength-filled, ready to follow any dictate of his mind.

They turned right, stepped through a side door, and Jean's tiny gasp of awe was ample reward for all that Curt had done.

The air was warm and moist, heady with the oxygen of growing plants. Great tiers of water tanks rose along the walls, their surfaces thick with the green and yellow and bright colors of fruits and vegetables growing in the vitamin-charged hydroponic baths. They seemed to grow visibly, even as the Earthpeople watched.

Pipes as thick as a man's arm, bank upon bank, were braced in rows through the center of the immense room, and thousands of clear bubbles of water clung to them. The light of gravitic-stasis bulbs glowed deep in each bubble, and the surfaces of all were threaded with the tender shoots of growing seedling plants.

"How utterly incredibly marvelous!" Jean whispered.

The Falcon nodded proudly. "Ten thousand tons of food go out of this cavern every day, taken to the starving people of a dozen worlds. It is not a one man job; it is a tremendous task for hundreds of thousands of men and women." He pointed to the workers between the rows. "Those are the ones who are doing the job; those are my people, my friends. They and all people like them are what I fight for."

"It's gallant," Jean admitted slowly. "But it's also so incredibly foolish. A few hundred thousand, or even millions, cannot change the world we live in. It is far better to take things as they are." She shuddered involuntarily, as a snake-man glided effortlessly across the path. "After all, creatures like that shouldn't be permitted to live like Earthmen."

The Falcon shrugged, some of the good feeling going from his mind. Then he plucked a handful of rich dark grapes.

"Try these," he said. "We've still a lot of sightseeing to do."

For another hour they walked and talked, meeting the men and women with whom the Falcon worked. Nowhere was there a fawning attitude because he was the one whose word was law. There was a tangible feeling of equality among all the people, a feeling that the girl had never seen anywhere before.

She spoke but little, until she saw the great storeroom where the wealth of a hundred nations was piled in orderly stacks. She saw that the door had neither lock nor bolt, and her eyes were startled when she glanced at the tall man at her side.

"There's no need," he said, understandingly. "This is communal property. And there are no thieves in the Base. Anyway, if a thief did appear, he could not escape—an inertia-tractor beam would bring any ship back before it could get away."

Jean nodded, and they strolled toward the exit that led to their apartments. Neither spoke now; both were silent with their thoughts. A vocoder light was on at a corner box, and the Falcon flicked the switch.

"Yes?" he said quietly.

"A report has just come in, sir," the mechanical voice said evenly. "The girl whose ship you stole is—"

The Falcon whirled, feeling the ripping of his dis-gun from his holster. He whirled in a sudden spin that almost caught Jean Harlon; and then he came to a sudden halt, the last words of the vocoder ringing in his mind.

"—Jean Vandor, the daughter of Jason Vandor, the Food Administrator. She was attending a dance given by—"

The Falcon moved with a desperate tigerish speed, his hand lancing out to snatch the menacing gun. Then the softened ray caught him squarely in the chest, and the world blanked out.

He came to slowly, then with a rush of surging emotions that were like icewater to his brain. He rolled to his feet, wobbled unsteadily for a moment, then darted down the tunnel, running toward the comptroller's office. Tunnel after tunnel passed behind him, and he could feel the ragged pounding of his heart, as he raced across the last few yards of the entrance room.

He slammed through the door of the office, felt dismay and anger fill his mind when he saw the dissed wreck of the tractor beam board. Then he knelt, helped the comptroller to a chair, where the man sagged groggily.

The man shook his head. "The girl you came with burst in, demanded to know which were the tractor controls. I wouldn't tell, but she must have known, for she rayed them, and then blanked me out."

The Falcon snarled a curse. "She's a *telepath*," he said. "She read your mind." He whirled to a window, peered at the rocket runway that led into the escape tube. "One ship is gone," he finished harshly. "Without a tractor to bring her back, she'll take the news straight to her father. We can't fight the IP with half-gunned ships. I'll have to run her down."

"Your ship's been refueled and is ready to go. New radi-batteries are in the tractor gear." The comptroller roused himself with an effort.

"You sure you're all right?" Curt asked anxiously.

"I'm fine."

"Then tell Schutler and Crandal where I've gone. Tell them my orders are to triple the men outfitting the ships. I'll be back as soon as I can—but no move is to be made without my okay. Understand?"

"Yes, sir."

The Falcon whipped about, darted from the office. He ran at top speed, fitting the dis-gun he had grabbed from a wall rack into his belt holster. He raced to the conveyor belt, slipped into a seat, flipped the control to high speed. An instant later, he was hurtling toward his cradled ship, wind sighing past his face.

"Damn all women!" he thought. "Especially this one!"

The walls whizzed by in a grey blur, and thirty seconds later the conveyor jarred to a bone-shaking stop. Curt flipped the safety belt aside, dashed for the small cruiser resting in the cradle. He impatiently brushed aside a slow-moving workman, stepped through the port. He closed the port entrance, screwed it shut with powerful heavings of his shoulders, then darted to the control cabin. Sinking into the seat, he automatically checked the controls.

"Clear ways," he snapped into the vizi-screen, waited for the "all clear" signal. A green light flashed to his right, and he closed five stud switches in close succession. The ship lurched slightly, steadied, then fled with a rush of displaced air.

The inertia gate closed behind the ship, and the entrance hole flowed open. Ahead was the empty blackness of space. The next instant, the planetoid was far behind, and speed was piling at a terrific rate. Curt was grateful then to the man who had invented the stasis force-screen, for at the initial acceleration he had achieved, he should have been dead. But with all atoms of the ship and its contents building speed at the same rate, he felt no discomfort.

He bent toward the vision-port, scanned the Void with slitted eyes. Stars gleamed with a cold brightness far away. The Sun was at his back, and far to his right whirled Earth and Mars. Venus and Mercury fled their celestial ways far below and behind him.

He swore lightly, built up power in the vision-port, sent a scanner beam whirling. He missed the stolen ship on the first round of the beam, caught it on the second try. It was nothing but a tiny spearhead of yellow flame far ahead.

The rockets drummed with an increasing roar and muted vibration, as his fingers flicked the switches and studs before him. And despite the stasis-field, he felt the slightest sensation of travelling at an incredible rate of speed.

The freight ship was obviously moving at top speed, and was fully eighty thousand miles away. It fled in a parabola, travelling above the plane of the ecliptic, its speed now so great that it could not make a sharp turn so as to double back to Earth at Jean Vandor's touch on the controls.

Curt grinned. His ship was a cruiser, built for speed, a model that could outrace the other within a few minutes. He flicked close the last switch, sank back in his seat, watching the freight ship gradually drawing closer. He lit a *pulnik* cigarette, waited, knowing there was nothing else that he could do for moments.

Then he frowned, leaned forward. His hands grew white on the control board from the stress of his emotions, and he felt dull panic striking at his heart. For the freight ship had swerved, had swung about in an abnormal way, its rocket flow spinning in a flaming arc.

Curt watched with the sickness eating at his heart, for he knew what had happened. Inexperienced as she was, Jean had permitted her ship to be caught within the conflicting tides of gravity in space, and even now was being pulled in the Sargasso of Space.

She could not escape; there was no record of anybody ever escaping the tides. Her only hope lay in Curt Varga, the tractor rays of his cruiser, and the superior power of his ship.

He watched the futile struggle of the girl to tear the freighter loose, saw the ship whip about in a series of surging dives and evolutions that finally ceased as the ship slowly but surely was dragged into the midst of the whirlpool.

And now the two ships were but a few thousands of miles apart. Already, the gravity streams were tugging at the cruiser, striving to turn its flight into a diving plunge for the maelstrom's heart. Curt worked with a desperate calculating intensity, playing the power of the ship against the tides, as a master machinist judges the power of his tools.

He sent the cruiser to the left, flicked on the tractor ray, flashed its probing beam toward the freighter. The beam caught, whipped by, then flicked back. Curt could feel the instant tugging. He increased power, felt the shrill whine of the ray-machine building icy fingers in his brain. Then the sound was past the audible.

The tides swept over the cruiser, flipped it about like a leaf in a breeze, almost caused him to lose contact with the freighter. But the shimmering thread of the tractor's light did not break; the ships were locked together.

Curt coaxed the last bit of power from his rockets, sent his ship in a spiralling drive for free space. He smiled thinly, grimly, when the tossing of the cruiser lessened. He glanced from the vision port, wondering if they would get free.

A smashing blow struck the ship, drove it back, set metal to singing. Curt swore harshly. Space was filled with floating debris captured by the gravitic tides. Small chunks of meteoric rock flashed by, followed by clouds of dust as fine as gravel. The bloated, ruptured body of a space-ship rushed by in the opposite direction, hurled nowhere in its constant swinging about the area of dead space. Curt winced, when he caught the starshine on the bulgered bodies that trailed in its wake like a meteor cloud. He wondered, irrelevantly, who the men were.

And then from the darkness of space came a great sweeping clot of debris, the gutter rubbish of the space lanes. Ships that had been caught in the tides, meteors, rocks, all the flotsam that had been gathered through the ages.

But Curt had no time for that. He felt his ship winning free, sent it whipping to the left again, wondering if his rockets would burn out under the stupendous strain. And relief filled him, when he realized that he was pulling the other ship from its death-bed of gravity.

And even as he laughed, he felt all power cease in his ship.

He swore brittlely, fought with the controls. All of them were dead. Panicky, he stared from the vision port, and dull wonder filled his mind.

Twin tractor-beams were lancing from the clot of space debris below the ship, each centered on a different ship. The beams were almost white in their intensity, so great was their power.

"What the hell!" Curt Varga said audibly, relaxed momentarily.

And then the cruiser was hurtling toward the clot, sucked there by the tractor beam, moved with an incredible titanic force such as was only possible from a mighty generator. Curt swerved his gaze to the freighter, saw that it, too, was trapped.

He thought then of the words that his brother had spoken to him on Mars before, of the information that had come through about the base of the drug-smuggling ring being in the Sargasso. He cursed the utter blind stupidity that had made him discount the words even as they were spoken. And then puzzlement grew within him, for it was an established fact that, once caught within the Sargasso, nothing could escape. How, then, could this be the *smothalene* smuggling headquarters; the smuggling ships could not escape the drag of the knitted gravities?

But he had no more time for thinking. The cruiser jarred squarely into the center of the clot of debris, was sucked through it. Metal jarred and strained, and a light flickered into life on the board, indicating that a plate had been sprung in number Three hold.

Curt darted for the wall closet, unzipped it, tugged at his bulger. He slid into it, closed it, left the quartzite face-plate open until the control room was actually ruptured and the need for air from the shoulder tank was necessary.

Outside, rubbish flashed by the ports in a rush of whirling objects. Except for the crash and clatter of the cruiser forcing its way through the churning maelstrom, there was no sound.

The cruiser landed with a jar that threw Curt to one side, dazing him for a moment. He braced his feet, flipped a dis-gun from the wall rack, went slowly toward the port. He heard it unscrewing before he got there, and he cogged his head plate shut, switched on the flow of oxygen. The port came open, and a radio signal buzzed within Curt's helmet. He felt the rushing of air from the ship into the Void.

"Come on out, with your hands up," a heavy voice snapped authoritatively.

The Falcon paused irresolutely, then shrugged, shoved the dis-gun into a pocket of his bulger. Bending a bit, he stepped from the port, was menaced instantly by five dis-guns held in the hands of bulger-suited Earthmen. The leader moved forward, disarmed Curt, stared at him through the face plate of his spacesuit.

"I've been hoping we'd meet," he said in surprise. "But I never figured you'd come popping in like this!" He gestured about. "I'm Duke Ringo; these are some of my men."

Curt gazed about, recognized that he stood in the freight hold of a great liner. The metal was twisted and torn with gravitational strain, with only one wall intact. Even now, he was being herded toward that wall.

"I'm Davis, Kemp Davis," Curt said slowly. "I've been scavenging the lanes. I was trying to save that freighter, figuring salvage rates, when your ray brought me in." He affected a dead-face expression. "What are you men doing here, were you sucked in by the tides?"

Duke Ringo laughed scornfully. "To hell with that stuff, Falcon!" he said. "We know who you are; some of us have seen you. And we've got a—" He broke off, swung about to face another group clambering into the hold. "Who is it?" he snapped.

Curt's heart missed a beat; he took an instinctive step forward, stopped before the menace of a dis-gun. He heard Ringo's voice echoing tinnily in his earphones, heard another man's answer.

"It's a *girl*, Duke."

"Who, damn it!"

Jean's voice came dear and cool. "I'm Jean Vandor, daughter of Jason Vandor. If you have charge of these men, make them take their hands from me."

The second group slowly approached the first. The girl evidently recognized Curt, for her voice held a triumphant ring. "I see you've captured him," she said. "That's good. The reward for him will make all of you men rich. He's Curt Varga, Chief of the Food and Smothalene Pirates."

"Who'da thought it!" Duke Ringo said in mock amazement, turned away. "Come on, we'll get back to where it's comfortable."

"Nice going, Jean," Curt Varga said bitterly. "Because of your sheer stupidity, we're in a jam that made your former one look infantile. These boys are part of the *smothalene* smugglers; we haven't got a chance."

"Shut up, Varga," Duke Ringo said curtly.

Curt subsided, went slowly forward. They entered a small compression compartment, and Duke cogged a door shut. Air hissed from vents in the walls, and the pressure gradually mounted. Thirty seconds later, Duke Ringo unzippered his suit, motioned for the others to do the same. He lifted a box from one corner of the chamber, handed small nitration masks about.

"Stick these on," he said to Curt and Jean. "Otherwise you may find yourself aging pretty rapidly."

Curt fitted his mask to his nose, clamped his lips, his eyes flicking over the group of men. They were tough, as tough as any men he had ever seen in space. And he felt queasiness in his stomach when he saw the sheer cold brutality in their eyes when they looked at him. His fists tightened when he saw the manner in which they regarded Jean.

"All right, Ringo," Curt said. "Now what's the play?"

Duke Ringo turned slowly. He was fully as tall as Curt, but he was bulkier, heavier. He surveyed Curt deliberately out of expressionless eyes, then turned his gaze to Jean.

"The young lady," he said, "will be confined to a cabin for a few days. You, I think, will earn your keep by working at a drier."

A smuggler laughed openly, subsided when Curt spun toward him.

"I'm making no threats," Curt said finally. "But don't go looking for trouble. My men know where I am; they'll be looking for me. You can't afford to buck them."

Duke Ringo chuckled. "Don't be childish, Varga," he said. "Your men wouldn't have a chance in the tides; I only found out how to enter and get back, by accident. Play nice, and you won't get hurt. Try getting tough, and—" He spread expressive hands.

Curt took a stubborn step forward. "Listen, Ringo," he said earnestly, "my work is important; I've got to get back. I'll make a deal with you."

Jean pushed forward. "I'll *double* any bribe he offers you," she told Ringo, "if you keep him a prisoner for the IP. And I'll *triple* the reward, if you get me back to Earth within the next six days."

"Tsk, tsk, tsk!" Duke Ringo clucked his tongue. "Maybe I'll collect a reward bigger than you think—for turning both of you in later."

"How much ransom?" the Falcon said resignedly.

Duke Ringo pondered. "Not much," he admitted. "I just want to take over your base, your ships, your food-supply." He grinned, opened and shut his hands. "It looks as if I will."

Curt leaned forward, drove his right hand with every bit of strength in his rangy body. He forgot the issues at stake, in the blind rage of the moment; he thought only of his dreams he saw shattered beneath the grinding heel of the other's desire. He slashed with a desperate fury, and skin split on the knuckles of his hand.

Duke Ringo went sprawling backward upon the wall, a thin trickle of blood oozing from a swelling mouth. He swore nastily, came blasting forward, his right hand catching Curt high on the chest, his left darting in, smashing at Curt's jaw. Curt rolled with the punch, sagging backward, then side-stepping. He lashed with both hands, felt a blind gladness in him when his fists drew gasps of pain from the other. He waded forward, both hands pistoning, taking blows to his own face that sent curtains of red pain spinning through his brain.

And then a savage driving punch caught Duke Ringo squarely in the throat. He sagged, pawed with both hands at his battered larynx. He gasped, unable to speak, his face purpling from the effort to breathe.

Curt darted in, flicked out a hand, caught the exposed dis-gun at Ringo's belt. He flipped the gun free, whirled, menaced the remaining men with its flaring muzzle.

"Back," he snarled, "or I'll cut you down." He nodded at Jean. "Get behind me," he finished savagely. "This is our only chance to get free." He was the Falcon then, deadly, dangerous, a light burning in his eyes.

Jean moved hesitantly toward Curt, edged around him. The smugglers said nothing, apparently waiting for the slightest opening in Curt's offensive. Duke Ringo straightened, his face puffed, air whistling into his bruised throat.

"You'll never make it," Ringo said harshly. "Put down that gun."

Curt laughed mockingly. "I'll take my chances," he said.

And went cold with horror. For Jean lunged forward, swept the gun aside, and clung panting to his arm. The next instant, Duke leaned forward, and clubbed with his knotted fist. The blow caught Curt in the temple, hurled him to one side. He tried to turn, to spin, even as he was falling, but the girl's clutch on his arm tripped him. He went to his knees, his free hand shoving at the floor.

And then two of the smugglers had dropped on him, were smashing with heavy fists. Curt drew his legs beneath him, tore his arm free, came hurtling upward. In the midst of the movement, he saw the boot lashing at his face. He sobbed deep in his throat, knowing the blow could not miss. He tensed the muscles of his neck, rolled his head. And the boot smashed just below his right ear.

He felt the coolness of the metal flooring on his face, but there was only a grey blankness before his eyes. He tried to force his body to his feet, but there was no strength in his arms.

"Take him below," he heard Duke Ringo say. "Stick him at a drier. And because he likes to play tough, we'll see just how tough he is. *Make him work without a mask*."

The Falcon called out, but his voice was only a whisper in his mind. He felt oblivion reaching for him with talon-like fingers, felt panicky terror constricting his heart. He knew what the last order meant; and horror filled his brain. Then hands gripped his body, swung it high. He tried to fight, and the entire world collapsed in a blaze of white-hot light.

IV

The Falcon was drunk, completely, hilariously drunk. He sang a song about a girl with golden hair who rode a moonbeam in a race with the Venusian express, and he stopped now and then to breathe deeply, completely oblivious of the glances given him by the guards patrolling the catwalks above the manufacturing room.

He pressed the slender shoots of *lanka* weed into the cutters, drunkenly raked the chopped remnants into a basket. Lurching, he turned to the great kiln drier, dumped the basket load into the hopper, and closed the door. He adjusted the rheostat until a needle backed another on a dial, then went back to the cutter. He leaned against the machine, idly scratched the back of his neck with one hand, gazed blearily about the room.

Then he slipped several vitamin and energy capsules from his pocket and swallowed them. He felt their quick power sealing through his body, felt the cloudy numbness lifting from his brain. He fought with a desperate effort to think clearly and concisely, for he knew that another few weeks in the *smothalene* factory would kill him.

He waited patiently, felt strength coming back to his mind. Men watched him with a blind calm curiosity, their faces, behind their filtration masks, indicating their wonder that he should still be as well as he was after several days in the polluted air of the factory.

Duke Ringo had kept his threat; the Falcon had been compelled to work at thc *lanka* weed cutter without a mask. And those seven work periods had taken their toll of his rugged lithe strength. He was lucky that the machine filters permitted only the barest trace of the powder to get into the air, for a breath of the pure drug would kill him instantly, knotting his body with muscle-ripping cramps.

The drug, *smothalene*, was the deadliest aphrodisiac discovered in more than a century. Its action was swift and diabolic, raising the rate of metabolism to an incredible height, literally burning the flesh from the body of the users. Such was its action, the user consumed fifty times his normal usage of oxygen, and consequently went on an oxygen-drunk that was more satisfying, more habit-forming, than any drug that could be found. Its final effect came in a spasmodic, hideous moment, when the cumulative effects of the drug literally exploded in a surge of unleashed power. Every bit of energy and life was sucked from the body, and the corpse became nothing but a desiccated mummy.

The Falcon thought of that and many things, remembering the brushes his men had had with the smugglers, recalling the bodies of the *smothalene* users he had seen. And he remembered, too, the accusations hurled at him and his brood, wild accusations that placed him and his men in the roles of mass murderers—as the *smothalene* smugglers.

He gripped the machine edge tightly with whitening hands. He could feel the life being burned from his body from the tiny bit of the drug his body had assimilated, sensed the coolness coming to his heated muscles as the energy tablets fed the speeded metabolism. He knew instinctively that he had not grown so accustomed to the drug that he could not break its lecherous hold. All that he needed was a greatly supplemented diet for the next few days, and then, except for the natural deterioration of his body during the *smothalene* binge, he would be as perfectly conditioned as before.

A guard leaned over the edge of the catwalk, gestured with a paralysis gun. "Snap into it, Varga," he roared. "Your period isn't up yet."

The Falcon nodded, lifted new weeds into the hopper. Benton, the Earthman working at his side, flicked his gaze warily at the guards, and his voice was a quiet whisper.

"Don't be a sap, Falcon," he said. "Walk into a paralysis ray, get it over with in a hurry."

Curt Varga shook his head. "Sorry," he said softly, "I've got other plans."

Benton smiled derisively. "Yeah? Well, a couple of others thought they had, too. They got a converter burial in the energy room."

The Falcon swayed a bit, felt drunkenness creeping into his mind again. He found and swallowed the last of his energy tablets.

"Look," he said, "I need the help of everybody in here. I've got a plan that might work—but this *smothalene* is burning me so I can't really think. Collect all the energy tablets the men can spare for me; I'll use them to stay sober until I bust the place wide open."

Benton shook his head.

The Falcon raked weeds into the cutter, glanced about.

"The guards think I'm drunk all of the time," he whispered. "They don't worry about me any more; I can do damned near as I please. Get me those energy tablets, so my mind won't blank out at the last moment, and I'll guarantee freedom for all of us."

The Earthman considered gravely for a moment, then nodded doubtfully. "I'll do what I can, Falcon, only because of your reputation. If your idea doesn't work, there's little lost, anyway."

Slowly, he turned, caught up a great oil-can, drifted among the machines. He talked quietly with worker after worker, finally returned and handed Varga a double handful of tablets.

"That's all I could get," he said. "Now what happens?"

"Watch for your cue." The Falcon dropped the tablets into his pocket, retaining about a dozen. He swallowed them, felt their cool rush of energy almost immediately. He unscrewed a vial from beneath a jet.

Then he proceeded to get very drunk.

His face went slack, his muscles rubbery. He sang in a cracked tenor, weaved carelessly through the machines, going toward the steps that led to the catwalk. He staggered drunkenly, almost belligerently righted himself again and again.

"Get back to work, Falcon," a guard called, grinned at the slackness of the pirate's once-erect body.

"I don' wanna work!" Curt Varga said nastily. "I'm gonna be sick."

"All right!" The guard jerked his head toward the rest-room. "Be sick, and then get back to your job." He grinned, as the Falcon came laboriously up the stairs.

The Falcon staggered drunkenly toward the rest-room, shoved through the door, dropped his pretense the moment he was alone. He went swiftly toward the air-intake grill, worked at its fastenings with a screwdriver secreted in his boot-top. And as he worked, he thought.

"*Jean*," he thought, and his face went white from concentration. "*Jean, this is the Falcon. Listen to me. In a few minutes, I'm going to release smothalene into the air-system. Put on your mask, and be ready to run for it.*"

He sent the message again and again, wishing that he had had the telepathic training to receive as well as send. He had no way of knowing if the girl could get his message; he had no way of knowing whether or not she would tell Duke Ringo of his plans.

The grill plate came loose in his hands, and he lifted the vial of *smothalene* powder into the hole revealed. For a second, his hand remained there, and then he felt the sickness of futility come over him. He had no mask.

He stepped back from the wall, pocketed the vial, went toward the door. He hesitated for a moment, then pulled the door ajar, beckoned drunkenly to the nearest guard.

"Cummere," he said melodramatically. "I got somethin' to show you."

"What's the matter?" the guard asked suspiciously, and his gun was bright in his hand.

"Thieves, that's what it is," the Falcon asserted solemnly. "Cummon, I'll show you."

He opened the door wide, turned his back, walked toward the gaping grill-hole. The guard entered suspiciously.

"All right," the guard said. "What's up?"

"See!" the Falcon said, pointed.

The guard gaped. "Who in hell did that?" he swore angrily. "Now I've gotta—" He swung about, momentarily forgetting the man with him.

The Falcon swung with a delicate precision, striking with the death-blow of a trained IP agent. The guard was dead before his sagging body was caught in the pirate's strong arms. He never moved.

The Falcon laid the body gently on the floor, removed the filtration mask, fitted it to his face. He pulled the coat from the slack arms and shoulders, carried it with him to the wall. Carefully, he emptied his vial of the *smothalene* crystals into the air-tube, covered the hole with the muffling coat. He stood that way for several minutes, until he was certain that the dust had been carefully sucked along the pipe. Then he darted back to the guard, took his gun, and stepped to the door.

He shot the approaching guard squarely through the throat, the gun singing its piercing note of death, the instant cry of the guard disappearing with his throat. Then the Falcon hurdled the body, raced along the catwalk.

"Benton," he yelled, "*this is it.*"

A guard shouted in brief anger, his ray searing a burning streak of agony along Curt's side. Then the Falcon whirled, dropped to one knee on the metal flooring, and his gun sang a song of death that didn't cease.

Rays lanced from the patrolling guards, and their cries were startled angry sounds. One went down from the Falcon's ray; another lined his gun with a deliberate slowness.

A thrown spanner-wrench crushed in the side of his head, and Benton raced up the catwalk's steps. He waved two more wrenches at the Falcon.

"Let's go, Varga," he shouted.

The Falcon rayed the last two guards to death with a single sweeping shot that cut them down as though before a scythe. Then he was running toward the exit.

"Stay here and organize the men," he yelled back. "Follow as quickly as possible, and mop up the smugglers still alive."

Then he had plunged through the door and was racing down the corridor. He gagged in sheer horror when he saw the bodies of the smugglers in the hall and adjacent rooms. They were sere and brown, withered mummies dressed in clothes sizes too large. Some still twitched feebly in their last throes. *Smothalene* had dropped them with their first deep breaths of the virulent drug.

He raced on, his feet pounding deafening echoes from the floor, his gun gripped tightly in his hand. He prayed silently as he ran. And then he was at the control cabin, skidding to a stop, his gun swivelling to menace the room. It was empty, except for the sere mummy of a man at the astrogation table.

"Damn!" the Falcon swore, swerved about as a footstep sounded at the door. Then he was holding Jean in his arms, soothing the shaking of her slender shoulders.

"Ringo escaped!" the girl cried. "He was making me broadcast a ransom demand to my father, when I got your message. I grabbed a mask, and ran. He must have suspected something, for he didn't chase me. I hid, and watched him running toward the escape hatch. He was wearing a bulger." She glanced at the mummified man at the table, shuddered, tears flooding her eyes.

The Falcon shoved her aside, sprang to the control board. He flicked a switch, grinned tautly when a needle leaped to instant life. He sat in the seat, laid his gun aside. Flicking on the vizi-beam, he sent its scanner ray swirling about outside the dead ship. Almost instantly he found the tiny cruiser boring toward the outside of the clot of space debris.

His hands darted to two levers on the board, drew them back. Tractor rays leaped into sudden life, spun in pursuit of the fleeing cruiser. Secondary rays fended off the rubbish that tended to be sucked into the tractor beams.

Then the tractors caught the cruiser, caught and held it immovable. It swung about, almost stopping its direct flight. It bucked and plunged like a fish on a line, rockets flaring with incredible power to break the hold. But Curt's hands never gave it a chance. The rays grew whiter by the second, became almost invisible in their power. And the cruiser wheeled over, began sinking slowly toward the headquarter's ship.

The vizi-screen grew silvery, then green, and a face appeared on its surface.

"Clever, weren't you, Falcon," Duke Ringo said viciously. "I should have killed you when I had the chance." His eyes were mad pits of reddish hell. "I knew something was wrong when the girl made a dash from me with a mask, but I didn't have time to warn the men, for I wasn't certain what was happening. Then the *smothalene* dropped my mate, and I barely got into a bulger before I had to take a breath. I had to run for it; I couldn't have fought your entire crowd."

The Falcon's face was stony and bleak, his eyes impersonal.

"I'm bringing you back, Ringo, and turning you in."

"To hell with you, Falcon," Duke Ringo snarled. "When I go out, you go, too." He laughed. "*All right, I'm coming in!*"

The vizi-screen went momentarily black, then the scanner ray cut back in. Duke Ringo's ship had ceased its futile efforts to escape; now it was turning, the needle prow centered directly on the smuggling headquarters. In that one flashing second, the Falcon felt a surge of admiration for the brutal bravery of the man.

But there was no time for thinking; there were only a few seconds in which to act with an instinctive blinding speed. Duke Ringo's ship was smashing downward now, driving at full-speed throttle, speeding with the combined power of the tractor rays and the surging drone of its rockets. It flashed with a speed that increased by the second, became a diving bullet that could not miss its mark.

Curt Varga cursed deep in his throat, switched off the tractor beams, watched the ship smashing in. He cringed from the explosion he knew was coming, felt terror deep in his mind. Then sanity reasserted itself, and his hands moved with a flowing speed.

He flicked on the tractor rays again, sent them spiralling to one side. They touched a fifty-foot meteor, caught it, spun it into the path of the hurtling death-ship.

Duke Ringo tried to swerve the cruiser, failed, for the ship and meteor struck in a titanic slanting blow. White heat flared for a soundless moment, force waves pushing outward in the burst of energy. Then the ship and meteor were one, and in their place was only a fused lump of metallic refuse that spun endlessly in the Sargasso of Space.

The Falcon cut all switches, turned slowly about on his seat. He stared at Benton and the other prisoners who had crowded into the room. He felt the nearness of the girl at his side, cursed himself for becoming a sentimental fool.

"The show's over," he said quietly. "Ringo's dead."

V

Fourteen hours later, the Falcon stood before the control board of his sleek pirate cruiser. Jean was at his side, and they faced the vizi-screen. Except for a certain amount of lethargy because of the tiny amount of drug he had inhaled in the *smothalene* factory, the Falcon felt all right again. He was dressed in fresh clothes, a new gun was buckled at his waist. And through the blackness of his hair were threaded bits of silver the past few days had brought. Jean was dressed becomingly in some of the Falcon's spare clothes, appearing much like a rather pretty boy playing in his father's garments.

"Benton and the others," the Falcon said, "have their orders and directions for finding the Base. Those of you who did not care to join me may go where your fancies dictate. Now, don't forget. To free yourself of the Sargasso, you merely have to hold your ships to the debris clot with a tractor, and race at full throttle in as large a circle as you can. When maximum speed is reached, cut the tractor, and centrifugal force will throw you free. Has everybody got that?"

Acknowledgments came piling in from the thirty ships gathered about the Falcon's ship.

"Then let's go," the Falcon said, and sat at the controls. He flipped switches, built up speed, finally cut loose, and the Sargasso fled back behind them.

The Falcon set the robot-control, sighed relievedly. He grinned at the girl beside him, liked what he saw in her eyes.

"I'm doing this against my better judgment, Jean," he said half-mockingly, half-seriously, "but since you've given me your solemn oath, I'm willing to take a chance. Anyway, you owe me your life; for that, you should be willing to keep the Base's location a secret."

Jean Vandor nodded. "I shall keep my word," she said slowly, then she sank into a seat, caught at the Falcon's arm. "Please, Curt," she finished swiftly, "please forget this mad plan of yours! I don't say you're right or wrong, I just say that the odds are too great for you to win. Come with me to Earth; my father will see that you are given a good job where you can be wealthy and respected. I promise you that."

The Falcon fashioned two *pulnik* cigarettes, handed one to the girl. He shook his head slightly, wryly.

"Sorry," he said, "but I couldn't, even if I wanted to. I owe too much to the people who trust me. And I have a certain sense of integrity that wouldn't let me sleep nights, should I quit now." He smiled with the quickening exuberance of a man ten years younger. "Put in a good word for me, though; I'll maybe need it, if things go wrong."

Jean Vandor smoked her cigarette silently. "They will go wrong," she said finally.

"It's a chance worth taking." The Falcon shrugged. "But tell me of Ringo's ransom demands; this is the first real chance we've had to talk, what with wrecking the smuggling headquarters, plundering the dead ships of the Sargasso, and then making our escape." He grinned. "I thank you for that, anyway; if you hadn't heard Ringo telling his men how to escape the gravitic tides, we'd be there, yet."

Jean nodded. "I heard him give the order when a new recruit was about to take a ship out. As for the ransom demand; well, Ringo demanded immunity from the Administrators, and a license to sell *smothalene* throughout the system, in return for my release. But as he told me, he planned to keep me prisoner until all the drug now manufactured was sold. With myself as a hostage, my father would be helpless to fight back."

The Falcon turned to the control board, made minute adjustments, tried to force a casual tone. He could feel the flush stealing upward from his open collar.

"What do you plan to do, once back on Earth?"

"Nothing, I suppose, just the things I did before—well, this entire affair happened."

"Are you—" The Falcon came to his feet, walked to the door. "Nothing," he finished. "I think I'll get a bit of sleep before we land."

Not waiting for a reply, he walked down the corridor. He hated himself at the moment, hated himself and the life he lead. In his mind grew the first nucleus of a doubt that he might be wrong. In all probability, what he should do, what was the logical thing to do, was to accept Jean's offer, forget his past, and try to settle back into the ordered routine of life the Administrator's plans had mapped for twenty billion people.

Entering his cabin, he threw himself on the bunk, smoked interminable cigarettes. And as the hours passed, coherence came to his thoughts, and the bitterness faded. After a time, he slept.

He woke only when the light tap came on his cabin door.

"We're landing, Falcon," Jean said breathlessly. "I talked with father, and he has promised a truce for the period you are on Earth."

"I'll be right out," Curt Varga said, felt the vague prickle of a premonitory thrill along his spine. Then he shrugged, climbed from the bunk, did quick ablutions. Five minutes later, his hand was on the controls when the cruiser glided to a landing at the spaceport.

Jason Vandor waited on the field, his purple robe bright in the midst of his personal bodyguard. He caught Jean in his arms, and the Falcon felt a certain sense of gladness when he saw the open affection of the man toward his daughter. Despite his faults, the man was truly a father.

"So you're the Falcon," Vandor said at last, staring at the pirate from eyes as blue and chill as ice.

Curt Varga grinned. "I'm the Falcon," he said calmly. "But I never thought to meet you under these circumstances."

"Nor I. But I do offer you thanks, anyway."

"You owe me nothing; I am here under truce. When I leave, our battle starts again."

Vandor smiled. "But you see, Falcon, that is where you are wrong. I thank you for bringing my daughter back, yes; but I also thank you for saving my men the trouble of running you down." His hand made a sharp imperative gesture. "*Blank him out*," he ordered.

There was no time to move, no time to think; there was only the split second of consciousness when he saw the smile of triumph on Vandor's face, and its mocking echo on the girl's. Then the dis-gun blast caught the Falcon squarely in its glow, sucked away all thought and dropped him into a blackened abyss that had no bottom.

The Falcon moved groggily, felt nausea cramping at his belly. He groaned, shook his head, forced himself erect. Chains clanked loudly, and he felt the coolness of their metal on his arms and legs.

"Hell!" he said feelingly, felt despair eating at his heart.

Jason Vandor moved slightly, sighed, then stood from where he sat across the cell. His grey hair was almost white in the gloom, and his face was hard and merciless.

"I want to talk to you, Falcon," he said harshly.

Curt Varga blinked away his dizziness, searched the cell with his eyes. Except for two bunks, it was empty. The chains he wore were welded to the bunk upon which he sat.

"Go ahead," he said finally. "You seem to have the whip hand."

"It's about Jean." There was a tiny thread of fear running through the dictator's voice.

"All right, what about her?"

"I want you to do something. She and I just had a terrible fight, the first I can remember having with her since she was a child. She seems to think that I was wrong in capturing you while I had a chance. Now, I know such a request is strange, I know you hate me, but I want you to talk with her, and convince her that I was in the right. You know our fight is to the death; you know that neither of us asks quarter; you know you would have done the same thing had you been in my place. I'm not asking this for myself; I'm asking for her peace of mind. Her life will be wrecked, if she hates me as long as she lives."

The Falcon laughed, and the sound was ugly and ironic in the semi-darkness. He had met strange situations in his years as a freebooter of space, but none of them had been as fantastic as this.

"You honestly mean that you want me, the man you intend to execute, to intercede for you with your daughter?"

Panic tightened Jason Vandor's voice. "I'll make it worth your while, Falcon," he said. "I'll see that you are not executed; I'll see that you get life. I'll even see that you have all requests granted."

"To hell with you," the Falcon said dispassionately.

"Falcon, you've got to listen to me, you've go to. Jean is a girl, she's been brought up differently than either of us. You and I know what fighting and death are; you and I have no illusions to temper our judgments—we are cold intellects. But Jean is young, she has ideals, and they must not be destroyed. You have appealed to her instincts for romance; she has colored your actions of the past few days until you seem to be what you pretend to be. Now I want you to make her understand that your real desire to crush me and the other Administrators has nothing romantic about it; you must make her realize your real purpose—that you plan to become dictator in the Administrator's place. Will you do that, Falcon?"

Curt Varga sagged back against the wall, stared blindly at the man before him. Thoughts were chaotic in his mind.

"You *believe* that, don't you, Vandor?" he said slowly.

"Of course, what else can I believe? Self-government, freedom, bah! The cattle of the worlds wouldn't know what to do with either."

The Falcon shifted. "Where is Jean?" he asked.

"On her way to Mars, where I sent her." Jason Vandor's tone grew harsh and strained. "I'm making a request, Falcon," he finished, "and I can be generous in return. But make me force you to talk to her, and I can do to you just what you would do to me." He laughed without mirth. "A pitcheblend mine, wearing no protection, might be much worse than agreeing."

Curt Varga nodded. "I don't understand you, fully. You're a merciless butcher—yet you think enough of your daughter to bargain with your enemy. But I'll do what you say—for my freedom."

Jason Vandor shook his head. "Not that," he said brittlely. "I have no desire to fight you a running battle until the final showdown. You're dead, as far as your past is concerned. But you have your choice of death; either a slow one in prison, or a hideous one in a mine. Either way, you will fight me no more."

"What would I say?"

"Practically nothing. She swore she would believe what I said, only if you told her that my statements were the truth. Tell her that over a vizi-beam, and I promise you a decent prison life."

"I've sampled your promises."

"I swear I shall not go back on my word. Jean is the only thing in life I love; I'll do anything for her." Vandor's words were bitter and brooding.

"All right." The Falcon nodded. "I'll speak your pretty little speech. Not for you; I wouldn't give you water in hell. But for Jean; who at least hates and fights cleanly and openly." He spat. "Now get me out of here before I change my mind."

Jason Vandor stepped forward, tossed a key into Varga's lap. His concealed hand came from beneath his robe, and a gun glinted dully in his fist.

"Cross me, Falcon," he said quietly, "and for every minute of mental torture you give me, I'll give you a year of the same."

The Falcon unlocked his chains, stood erect. "I'll speak your piece," he answered. "But don't make threats."

He walked before the menace of the gun through the open door, followed the line of radi-lights down the stone corridor. He felt nothing but a dull apathy within his mind, and he cared nothing for the future. He knew there was no escape, and the knowledge left him unemotional.

But then the thought came that Jean had fought on his side, and he felt warmness spreading through his heart. There was a gulf between them, a space that would never be spanned. Yet he felt closer to the girl now than he had felt toward any person other than his brother in years.

"This way, Falcon," Jason Vandor said.

They walked a corridor, turned right, entered the vizi-beam room where operators sat before the machines that connected with all planets.

Jason Vandor stopped beside a machine. "Get the *Ardeth* on the beam," he ordered.

"Yes, your Lordship!" The beam-man's fingers made clicking contacts with the machine's controls. The vizi-screen became silvery, slowly turned green.

Life grew on the screen. Color swirled, then merged, and Jean Vandor frowned from the screen.

"Yes?" she asked.

Jason Vandor forced the Falcon to the screen with his gun. The Falcon was conscious then of the utter quiet in the room, as though all were afraid to breathe. He could feel the pounding of his heart as he stepped forward.

"Can you hear me, Jean?" he asked quietly.

"I can hear you, Curt."

The Falcon forced all feeling from his voice. "Jean, answer me truthfully; did you plot that I should be captured?"

Tears welled in the girl's eyes, and her head shook slightly.

"No, Curt."

Curt Varga sighed then, and the ache in his heart was a tangible thing that hurt with an agony he had not thought possible for a man to feel.

"Remember the things I told you, Jean? Remember the hopes and dreams and plans I had?"

"I remember."

"Then, Jean, this is the truth. Remember this all of your life; fight for it, never let it die. *Men are born to be free; no man can place himself in the role of God, there to dictate what—*"

The blow of the gun barrel smashed him to his knees. He knelt there for seconds, laughing into Jason Vandor's face.

"I'm a *small* man, Vandor," the Falcon said. "I can hate and I can love. But I am true to myself, if nothing else. Get somebody else to do your lying."

Jason Vandor's face was a chiseled mask of evil rage. He saw then the crumbling of the life he had built, saw then the truth that lay in the Falcon. He knew then that all of the treasures and powers of a hundred worlds could not replace that which he had lost in those fleeting seconds.

He lifted his gun to shoot the defenseless Falcon to death—and died that way, a dis-ray scything him down in a huddled heap.

"By damn, a fight at last!" a great voice roared from the doorway, and Schutler sprang into the room.

His laughter was mad with the richness of the moment, and the twin guns were almost buried in the greatness of his fists. Crandal was at his side, his bald head gleaming, his gun lancing flame like a jet of glowing water. And behind both, shoving them forward, came Jericho, his ebony face agleam, a great sword in one hand, a gun in another.

"*Falcon!*" Jericho cried, and his gun made an arc through the air, was caught deftly in the Falcon's reaching hand.

Then hell broke loose in that great room, a hell of a dozen darting crossing rays of death, a holocaust of power that surged and twisted and searched for the lives of the men within.

A guard went down, his gun still holstered, his face blown away by the left gun of the laughing giant at the door. Crandal darted sideways like a crab, gun-flame licking out, precisely, almost daintily, never wasting energy on the wall or air. And Jericho moved like a black whirlwind, countering the dis-flame of a single guard by touching it with his sword-blade, and grounding the energy in his power-glove.

And the Falcon was on his feet, his laughter ringing as in the days of old, when a fight had been the thing to set a man's blood to pounding, when to live was a zestful thing of promise, when the future was bright and the past a gay memory.

He raced to the side of his men, cutting a guard from his side, raying a second even as he was lining his gun on Jericho. The Negro grinned, and his swinging sword fled through the neck of a guard, followed about and dropped a hand from the wrist of a screaming second.

Schutler went down, his beard flaming where a bolt had grazed his chin. He roared like an angry bull, pawed at the flame and smoke of his burning beard, swept his other hand as a man sprays water. Guards dropped like flies beneath a poison spray.

A shot caught Crandal in one leg, dropped him to his knee. His face went even whiter, and sweat was on his head.

The Falcon sprang to Crandal's side, caught him up with his left arm, raised a barrage of shots with the gun in his right. His teeth were white against the tan of his face, and the cold of his grey eyes was strange against the laughter that filled his face.

And the four were together, and no man could stand against them. They were courage and brains and strength and agility, all together, yet separate in themselves. Apart, they could be downed; but together, all hell itself brought mad rich laughter to their throats, and a flame to their eyes.

They stood together, and their guns made singing sounds that were like those from a harp of death. And before those notes men sank and died, one by one, and two by two, until only living stood beside the door, and there was no other life.

"Come, man," Schutler boomed, "before others hear the fight and stick their noses in!" He fingered the stubble of his beard.

"Are you all right, Jim?" the Falcon asked Crandal, and the man grinned with a white-faced smile.

Jericho caught up the wounded man, ignoring a ray burn that raced like a livid purple snake across the blackness of his shoulders. He jerked his head at the door.

"We come in by a secret passage," he explained in a rush of words. "We didn't find you in the cells, so we come hunting."

The Falcon choked back the lump in his throat, and his eyes were misty as he looked at the men to whom loyalty was neither a word nor a gesture, only a thing that was in them when the need arose.

"How—?" he began.

"I did it, Curt," Jean's voice said.

Jean was crying then, crying like a child whose first dreams are gone, crying like one whose new dreams are but the faintest of sounds in her consciousness. Through the vizi-screen she had seen all that had happened, and the sickness in her eyes would be long leaving.

"Jean," the Falcon said. "Please, Jean—"

She was smiling then, smiling through the tears that would not stop. And the Falcon, watching her features on the screen, knew the torture that was hers.

"I'll be waiting, Curt," she said. "But hurry—Oh, please hurry!"

"Wait for me, Jean, *wait for me.*"

And the Falcon and his brood were running down the hall, running toward the secret spot where a pirate ship waited to take them back to their fight and their loves and their freedom—and to the far horizons of their starway destiny.

Milton Keynes UK
Ingram Content Group UK Ltd.
UKHW050649260624
444769UK00004B/179

9 789362 092380